MAGIC JEWELLERY

G

An
Adventure

Written by Mick Gowar
Illustrated by Rob Chapman

HENDERSON
P U B L I S H I N G   L T D

Contents

1 Tate's Journal   5

2 Aboard The Antelope   25

3 The Ambush   40

4 Caught in a Trap   58

5 Squanto to the Rescue   66

6 Surrendering the White Flag   77

7 The Letter   88

1. Tate's Journal

"You're in my part of the seat!" snapped Katie.

"Am not!" Gemma snapped back.

"Are too!"

"Ow!" shrieked Gemma. Mum twisted around in the front seat of the car. "What's going on, you two?" she demanded.

"She pinched me!" protested Gemma.

"I didn't!"

"You did!"

"Well – you deserved it!" snapped back Katie. "Your hand was on my part of the seat!"

Simon, who had been sitting quietly, raised his eyes to the roof in despair.

Dad glanced up into the rear-view mirror. "*Please* stop bickering," he said. "I know it's been a long drive from the airport, but the back seat's plenty big enough for three people to share without squabbling." He paused. "We'll soon be there. Look! There's the sign: *Lakeside*

Pioneer Motel!"

"What's a pioneer when it's at home?" asked Katie, grumpily.

"Someone who is the first person ever to do something," replied Dad. "The motel is near where the first Europeans settled in New England. They were called the Peacehaven Pilgrims. They left Portsmouth in England to start a new life here in America."

"So why are they called Peacehaven Pilgrims and not Portsmouth Pilgrims?" asked Gemma, suddenly taking an interest in the conversation. She loved anything to do with the past.

"Good question," said Dad. "It's because they called their first village Peacehaven."

"Why Peacehaven?" asked Gemma.

"Because they were looking for a safe place – a haven – to practise their own religion in peace," explained Dad. "In those days, there were laws in England which said what you could and couldn't believe. The Pilgrims risked being thrown into prison because their beliefs were against the law."

"So they came here, to America?"

"Yes," replied Dad. "Here they could make their own laws, and worship as they wanted. But they didn't fly on a comfortable plane like we did. They came on a ship called *The Antelope*. Tomorrow we'll go to see a replica of *The Antelope* which is moored near the spot where the Pilgrims first came ashore."

Dad turned the car off the main road and steered along a bumpy track edged with thick evergreen woods. The track led into a clearing.

"Here it is!" announced Dad. "Our holiday home!"

The *Lakeside Pioneer Motel* looked less like a motel and more like a small village of log cabins, nestling among the birches and spruces of the thick Massachusetts woods.

They parked the car and followed the check-in signs to the largest cabin. A fat, balding man wearing a Boston Red Sox baseball shirt gave Dad the key to their cabin.

"If you follow the trail marked with green

arrows, you'll come to the lakeside," the man told them. "Real, unspoilt New England wilderness!" He had to shout to make himself heard over the thumps and grunts of the games machine in the corner.

The family clambered back into the car and drove down the woodland track to their cabin. They hauled their heavy suitcases out of the car and lugged them inside.

Gemma didn't bother to look around downstairs, but dragged her case up the stairs and into the bedroom she was to share with Katie. Making sure that no one was coming, she hurriedly unzipped the case and took out a travel bag. It had three compartments. Slipping her hand inside the back one she took out her magic jewellery box. Quickly, she opened it and checked; the necklaces were still there.

There was the sound of footsteps on the stairs and puffing, as if someone was straining with something heavy. Gemma stuffed the jewellery box under the pillow of the bottom bunk and lay down.

The door burst open. It was Katie,

dragging her bag behind her.

"Bags I have top bunk!" she shouted.

"You can have it," replied Gemma.

"Really?" asked Katie, incredulous.

"Sure," said Gemma. "I'm happy here."

While Katie started to rummage in her case, Gemma felt under the pillow to check that the box was safely out of sight. She'd found it in a cave when she'd been on holiday with her Uncle Mark who lived in Cornwall. The first time she'd put on one of the necklaces, she had found herself travelling through time and space, back to China in the time of mandarins and warlords; but she'd had to leave the necklace behind to get home.

There was a knock on the door and Simon ambled in. "There's one of those green arrows outside the cabin," he said. "I'm going to take a walk down to the lakeside – want to come?"

"All right," said Gemma.

Katie shook her head and pulled a computer game out of her case. "I'll stay here," she said, clambering up on to the top bunk.

Gemma and Simon followed the green arrows down a gently-sloping, red gravel path to the lakeside.

The lake was about half a kilometre across and one kilometre long. To the right was a small marina surrounded by a cluster of cabins built in the same style as the motel. The two children strolled around the shore towards the marina where there was a large cabin. A sign on the roof said: *Lakeside Pioneer Trading Post.*

"Come on," said Simon, "let's take a look inside." They walked up the wooden steps and through the door.

"Howdy!" called a cheerful voice from behind the counter. "Welcome to the Lakeside Pioneer Trading Post!" It was the fat man in the Red Sox baseball shirt who had checked them into the motel. "Our special offers today: fully washable, genuine Indian moccasins in 100% acrylic, only $9.95, and right above your heads, lady and gent, genuine Chippewa dream catchers, only $5.00 each or $9.89 for two!"

Gemma looked up. Hanging from one of the beams above her head were what looked like the heads of plastic badminton rackets, but without the handles and with most of the strings missing. She reached up and lifted one down for a closer look. Dangling from its rim was a large feather which had been dyed a sickly pink colour.

"Only $5.00...?" said the man behind the counter, hopefully.

"Er, no thanks," replied Gemma, putting it back.

"We got genuine Indian jewellery here, too," said the man, beckoning her over.

He reached under the counter and lifted out a large, glass-topped display box. Lying in the box were bead earrings, a couple of pendants hanging from leather thongs, and several thin, beadwork necklaces.

One of the necklaces in the display box looked familiar to Gemma. She stared at it hard. It looked a little like one of the necklaces in her magic jewellery box.

"These are real Indian necklaces, are they?" asked Gemma, looking up at the man.

"Yup," said the man. "All based on genuine Native American designs... Say, are you British?"

"Half-British, half-American," replied Gemma. She waited for the usual joke.

"Which half is American?" asked the man. "Top or bottom?" He laughed heartily.

"My dad's American," answered Gemma patiently. She pointed to the necklaces in the case. "So these were made by real – Iroquois, Huron...?"

The man looked distinctly uncomfortable. "Like I said – all based on genuine Native American designs. Say, you seem to know a lot about it for someone who's only half-American."

Gemma nodded. "Well, thank you for showing me the necklaces," she said politely.

"Don't you want to buy any?" asked the man, looking disappointed.

"Not today, thanks," replied Gemma. "...Or any other day," she added when she and Simon were safely out of the *Trading Post*.

"Wasn't it great!" exclaimed Simon. "While you were talking to the fat man, I was looking at the labels. The dream catchers came from Taiwan, the moccasins came from China, and the peace pipes were made in the Irish Republic!"

They plodded back up the gravel path to the cabin.

As soon as supper was finished and the dishes had been cleared away, Gemma went upstairs and got ready for bed. While Katie was in the bathroom, Gemma slid the magic jewellery box out from under her pillow and opened it. Lying on top of the necklaces was a string of tiny, coloured beads. Yes, thought Gemma, it does *look* Indian, but then so much at the Trading Post had looked Indian, too. She listened out for Katie's returning footsteps, but all was quiet. Tomorrow they were going to visit *The Antelope* and the Pilgrim Museum, where Dad had promised they would see *genuine* curios and artefacts. I'll take it with me and compare it with any Indian beadwork they've got there, thought Gemma. She slipped the necklace into the pocket of her jeans which were hanging over the back of the bedside chair. Then she slid the box back into its hiding place under her pillow.

By the time Katie came back into the room, Gemma was fast asleep on the bottom bunk with Melvin the moose clutched tightly under her arm, like an

American football in the arms of a running quarterback.

"Welcome to the Peacehaven Pioneer Village," said the woman in the crisp, light blue suit. "My name is Joanna Proctor, and I'm a direct descendant of one of the original families that sailed on *The Antelope*. I am your tour guide for today. Please follow me..."

She led the way up an immaculate street of spotless log cabins.

"This is an authentic reconstruction of the original Peacehaven village," she announced. "Everything is just as it was when the original village was founded in 1621!"

The family trudged around the village in an obedient crocodile behind their guide. She pointed out the smithy, the baker's shop and the home of the Tates – her ancestors.

As they reached the top of the main street, they were interrupted by a high-pitched bleeping noise. Joanna reached into her neat shoulder bag and pulled out a mobile phone.

"Yes..." she said. There was a long pause. "Oh...Oh no!...Oh *dear*!..." She switched the phone off and put it in her bag. She looked flustered.

"Is there something wrong?" asked Dad.

"A school party has arrived early," said Joanna, "but I haven't finished taking you around." She seemed at a loss as to what to do.

"Don't worry about us," said Dad, reassuringly. "Just show us the way to *The Antelope* and we'll be fine."

"If you're sure..." said Joanna uncertainly. She pointed ahead. "Just follow the path with the yellow arrows, and you can't miss it." Then she hurried back towards the main gate.

Gemma turned and gazed back down the main street. Although the guide had said that it was just as it had been in 1621, Gemma wasn't convinced.

"Do you think it was this clean and tidy – I mean, the real Peacehaven? It couldn't have been – could it?"

No one answered.

She turned back. The others had gone ahead. She ran to catch them up, jogging along the path that led down to a small cove by the sea. Alongside a plain wooden jetty was a tiny sailing ship with three masts, and a crowd of tourists standing nearby.

"Is that *it*?" asked Gemma.

"What's the matter?" asked Dad.

"I thought everything was supposed to be as it was in the settlers' days," said Gemma.

"It is," said Dad.

"But the ship's only a model – I mean, not a toy model, but it can't be full size."

"That's *exactly* the right size," said Dad.

"But last night you said that 102 Pilgrims sailed on *The Antelope*."

Dad nodded. Gemma stared at the tiny ship in disbelief.

They climbed aboard and inched their way down a narrow flight of steps, into the belly of the ship. It was dark and cool, and very, very small.

"Imagine what it must have been like," said Dad, thoughtfully. "102 Pilgrims, plus crew, all crammed into a tiny space like this. Sailing across the Atlantic for weeks and weeks; being nearly swamped by storms; everyone seasick..."

Mum shuddered. "They must have been very brave – or very desperate."

"They were both," said Dad.

Back on shore, they stood and gazed at the ship. It looked trim enough, with the gunwales and all the wooden facings around the stern cabin windows painted a dazzling white, and the gold-coloured antelope at the prow.

"Come on," said Dad after a while. "Let's go and visit the museum." He glanced at his watch. "We haven't got a lot of time if we want to get to Cambridge in time for lunch."

He led them back along the track between the dunes.

"It must have been awful being on board that ship," said Gemma. The car had seemed cramped to her, but 102 people crammed below deck on that minute vessel would have been a hundred – no – a thousand times worse.

"I don't think we can even imagine how dreadful, how absolutely terrifying, it must have been," said Dad.

They were all in a thoughtful, sombre mood as they filed into the museum. On a table by the door was a pile of brown booklets. Gemma picked one up: *A Short History Of The Peacehaven Community.*

I'll read this before I have a look around, thought Gemma, so I know what I'm looking at.

There was a little window seat in the entrance hall. She sat down and opened the booklet. She read about how the original settlers had come from England, and about how their ship had been blown off course. They had landed far to the north of where they'd intended to establish their settlement. She read about how they had found Indian corn buried in pits in the ground, and of the great sickness which killed almost half the settlers during the first winter. Finally, she read about how the survivors were saved by a friendly Indian, named Squanto. He spoke English because he had been taken to London as a kind of human curiosity many years earlier. Later, he had returned to America on a ship of hopeful settlers who had taken one look at the bleak, northern landscape and sailed south to the Carolinas.

Gemma stood up and tucked the booklet into the pocket of her jeans. Then she walked from the hall into the first room of the museum. She found herself alone in a large, airy room. Mum, Dad, Katie and Simon had moved on to the next room, but she didn't feel any need to hurry after them. The visit to the ship had put her in a quiet, thoughtful mood. The skylight in the roof filled the room with golden sunlight. Sometimes it was good to be alone.

In the centre of the room was a rough, home-made wooden cradle, and against the right-hand wall was a glass display case. Gemma walked over to the display case and looked inside.

In the middle was an old, handwritten book, and some old letters. Gemma looked at the small typed notice beside the book:

This book is the journal written by Nathan Tate, second Governor of Peacehaven, during the first ten years of the Peacehaven settlement.

Gemma had already read several extracts from Tate's journal in the brown booklet. The journal was open at a page dated December 1621.

My poor precious babe, Priscilla, is weaker still. Though she has not succumbed to the sickness, I do most greatly fear for her. We are very short of food, and though Captain Staunton and myself organise daily foraging parties, yet good fortune have we none. What will happen to all our little ones if we do not find food soon? We must all remain steadfast in our faith...

Gemma stared at the faded, spidery writing. Almost half of the colony had died in the first year, it said in her booklet. They had spent the winter searching for food but had found none. Weakened by starvation, half of them – men, women and children – had died in that dreadful first winter. If only they had known earlier about the corn in the pits, or that Squanto and the Indians could help them. She hoped against hope that the Tates' baby had been one of the lucky ones.

Gemma wandered over to the wooden cradle in the centre of the room. Beside it was a plaque fixed to the floor:

This was the cradle made by Nathan Tate for his infant daughter Priscilla, from the wood of the broken mast of The Antelope.

Gemma read the plaque again: *for his infant daughter Priscilla.* Was that a clue to what had happened to Priscilla Tate? Gemma wondered. *Infant* daughter – did that mean she'd never grown *beyond* being an infant – that she'd died as a baby?

Gemma turned away from the cradle. She wandered back to the diary in the glass case. She read the entry again, and then again:

We are very short of food, and though Captain Staunton and myself organise daily foraging parties, yet good fortune have we none. What will happen to all our little ones if we do not find food soon?

This wasn't make-believe, like the squeaky-clean, reconstructed village. This was real: real pain; real fear.

If only...she thought. If only Tate and the other settlers had known that there *was* food and help if they looked in the right places. If only...

"If only someone could have told them!" said Gemma aloud. Her voice echoed back from the wooden walls and wooden floor.

Gemma felt in her trouser pocket. The bead necklace was there – the one that looked like Indian beadwork.

Maybe she *could* do something. After all, she'd helped Chang and Koong-Shee on a previous adventure. But would it work this time?

I've got nothing to lose, thought Gemma.

If it doesn't work, they're no worse off. But if it does work...

She went back to the seat in the entrance hall. Through the open door she could see the cabins and main street of the reconstructed Pioneer Village. But can I get back to the *real* settlement? she wondered.

Closing her eyes, Gemma tried to block out everything except the one thought:

Peacehaven, December, 1621...

Peacehaven, December, 1621... She slipped the bead necklace over her head: *Peacehaven, December, 1621...* The cabins, the main street and the entrance hall turned into a wild, swirling blur and vanished. Gemma could hear a voice in her head, chanting,

You shall journey far and wide
Across Time's endless seas...

And as the voice chanted, Gemma felt herself falling down, down, down, down...

2. Aboard The Antelope

The dizzy, spinning sensation stopped. Gemma opened her eyes. The neat log cabins and tidy stores of the Pioneer Village had vanished; she was standing on a flat, sandy seashore.

It was late afternoon and the sun was sinking slowly into the sea. A bitterly cold wind was blowing across the narrow beach. The sky was covered with low, grey, thick cloud, and the sea was a bluer, slate grey. The wind was whipping the waves into a rolling, lashing fury that burst against the rocks and exploded into white spume. There was the smell of snow in the air.

Gemma was completely alone. The icy blasts seemed to cut right through her thin clothing; the intense cold made her fingers and toes ache. She hugged herself, but the cold seeped right through to her bones.

I must find somewhere to shelter, thought Gemma.

She scrambled over the low dunes. The

ground beyond the beach was sandy and covered with broad-leaved, coarse grass. Dotted in between the clumps of grass were patches of frozen snow and ice. The wind seemed even more bitingly cold on the upland than it had on the beach. Gemma pulled her cotton jacket tightly around her and, leaning into the wind, fought her way up the steep rise to the top of a dune.

Stopping at the highest point, she swept the hair out of her eyes. She had walked halfway across a sand spit and was facing the sea again, but this time the water was calmer in an enclosed bay. A kilometre or so from where Gemma was standing was a tiny three-masted sailing ship. She peered through the icy wind. There was no mistaking the leaping, carved figure at the prow. It was *The Antelope* – the genuine, original *Antelope* – but compared to the replica in the Pioneer Village the real ship looked like a wreck. There was no dazzling white paint around the stern, no gaudy gilding, and the mizen-mast had snapped off. Where there should have been the beginnings of a settlement a little way in from the shore, there was nothing.

Where's the village? Where are the people? thought Gemma desperately. The cold was making all the muscles in her arms and legs ache, and daylight was fading fast. A flake of snow caught in her eyelid, followed by another, then another, and another. The painful cold ate away at her elbows and knees, and made her teeth ache. Her fingers and toes were now completely numb.

Gemma stared helplessly at the ship. It was too far away to call for help, and she knew that she was in real danger. If she didn't find some sort of shelter soon, she could literally freeze to death. She turned and looked around her.

Beyond the dunes were thick woods. Perhaps I could shelter in them, she thought. Then she heard a howl. Then, from a different part of the woods, an answering howl.

Wolves! The forest was much too dangerous, but she had to shelter somewhere; she was close to collapsing.

Gemma looked around again, desperately. Only a small sand dune, half-covered with snow, offered even the slightest shelter. It was pathetically little, but perhaps if she cowered behind it there might be some relief from the biting wind.

As she staggered towards it, Gemma noticed that there was something strange about the dune. The shape was too regular, and there was something odd about the colour, too. Brushing the snow off the top she saw that it was made of wood; wooden planks bent and nailed together. It wasn't a sand dune at all, but an upended boat! Gemma walked slowly around it. On the far side it had been propped against a rock, and between the edge of the boat and the sand there was a gap which was just big enough for her to crawl through.

Gemma squirmed under the upturned boat. It wasn't very comfortable. There were several pairs of oars beneath it, and she found herself squashed into one small, dark corner.

She huddled into the tiny space and gripped her jacket around her. The sand beneath the boat was wet and cold, but at least she was sheltered from the wind. The aches and pains grew less as she began to warm up a little.

Suddenly, there was a sharp bang on the side of the boat, as if someone had slapped or kicked it.

"Sailors!" she heard a muffled voice complain. "Once again they have deserted us and slunk back to the ship in their own boat, leaving ours unguarded. What if it had been discovered by savages and dragged off, or holed? What would we have been able to do then – eh? Nothing! Absolutely nothing! We would have been completely at the mercy of the savages and the elements!"

Gemma would have crawled out as soon as she heard the voice, but it sounded so angry that she decided to stay where she was.

"So, where are the others?" asked a second voice, calmer than the first.

There was quite a long pause. "There," the first voice replied, "just coming around the headland."

"Does it look as if they have found any food?"

There was another long pause. "No," replied the angry voice, now sounding grave. "They are not carrying any game, nor anything else that I can see."

There was a long sigh. "Come, Captain Staunton," said the second voice wearily. "Let us get this boat righted, so we are ready to get away from this dreadful place as soon as the others arrive."

Gemma huddled into her corner in panic. Who were these men? And what would they do when they found her under their boat?

There was a grunt from the angry man, then a sudden blast of cold wind that made Gemma gasp as the long rowing boat was rolled over on to its keel.

She closed her eyes and squeezed herself into a ball.

"What the – ?" she heard the rough voice bellow.

Slowly, Gemma uncurled and opened her eyes. She found herself staring up into the dark barrel of a musket. It was being pointed at her by a short man with bright red hair and a bushy red beard.

"Tell me your name and business, lad, or – so help me – I'll blow your head off!"

"B-b-b-but –" stammered Gemma.

"Name!" roared the red-haired man.

"Easy, Captain Staunton." A younger, clean-shaven man put his hand on the red-haired man's shoulder to restrain him. "He's only a boy, and he's terrified and half frozen." The younger man turned to Gemma. "Best do as the captain says," he said gently. "Tell us who you are, and how you came to be under our boat, boy."

"Boy?" questioned Gemma. She looked down at herself. Her jeans, sweatshirt and jacket made her look like a boy, and the man who was facing her had shoulder-length hair almost the same length as her own.

"Boy?" she repeated.

"Do you think he's a halfwit, Mr Tate?" asked Captain Staunton suspiciously.

"We'll find out soon enough," replied Tate. "Here are the others. This is no place to be having an investigation. We'll take him on board and find out who he is and where he comes from. Into the boat with you, lad."

Gemma was pushed roughly into the bow section of the boat by the red-haired man. "You sit there," he snapped, "where I can keep my eye on you. Any knavish tricks from you and – " He slapped his right hand against the barrel of his musket. "Do you understand me, boy?"

Gemma looked up from where she was sprawled in the bottom of the boat. "Y-y-yes, sir," she stammered, from a mixture of cold and fear.

With only Gemma, Staunton and Tate to weigh it down, the other men pushed the boat off from the shore then leaped aboard. Tate took the rudder, while Staunton sat guarding Gemma. The others took the oars and rowed silently, their breath coming out in great, steamy gusts.

As they came alongside *The Antelope*, a rope ladder was dropped over the side.

"Up you go, lad," growled Staunton. "And don't forget – I'm right behind you!"

Gemma clambered awkwardly up the rope ladder. It was dark, the ladder was slippery with ice, and her numb fingers could barely keep their grip. She was hauled over the side by two men waiting at the top.

"Who's this?" asked one, as Gemma scrambled to her feet.

Staunton had climbed deftly up the ladder just behind her, and now stood next to her on the deck, still holding his loaded musket.

"That's what we're about to find out," he growled. "Take him below!"

Gemma was bundled through a hatchway and then down a narrow wooden ladder into the hold. As soon as she reached the bottom of the ladder, she pressed both hands over her nose and mouth. The stench was indescribable. She looked around, appalled. There were people lying everywhere – some on mattresses, others on the bare, wet boards. Many were groaning, while some – obviously in high fever – were calling out, or mumbling garbled gibberish.

Staunton and Tate hardly seemed to notice the appalling smell and the sick people.

"This way," said Staunton gruffly. They led Gemma over to the far corner of the hold, where a dim lantern was swinging from a nail.

"Out with it, boy!" snapped Captain Staunton. "Who are you, and how did you come to be under our boat?"

"I-I-I crept under it to shelter from the cold," replied Gemma.

She'd been desperately trying to think of some explanation on the journey over in the rowing boat, but she'd come up with nothing plausible. Magic was no excuse this time. These were Puritans; they believed in the evils of magic, and the devil. Gemma remembered a history lesson at school about the early settlements in New England. They'd watched a film called *The Crucible* which was all about witch-hunting. Anyone suspected of practising magic was condemned as a witch, thrown into prison and executed! Gemma shuddered.

Tate intervened. "Did you come from a ship? Were you wrecked, or left behind?" he prompted gently.

"Y-yes," said Gemma uncertainly.

"Well – which?" demanded Staunton.

Gemma paused, desperately trying to

think of a believable story.

"Well – ?" repeated Staunton.

"I came ashore. I fell down – er – and when I woke up, I was all alone on the shore."

It sounded really weak and stupid, but in a way it was true. Gemma looked at Staunton; he obviously didn't believe her.

"Were you attacked?" asked Tate.

"Er – I don't know," said Gemma feebly. "I – I – " she paused. "I must have hit my head."

Tate nodded. "I have heard of such cases before, Captain Staunton," he said slowly. "A blow to the head, and all memory of the past is gone."

Staunton snorted, but didn't say anything.

"But apart from the blow, you are able-bodied?" asked Tate.

Gemma nodded.

"Then we must thank God that he has sent us a lad who is fit and strong, when we have such need," said Tate. "Ah! There is my wife – " He pointed to a tall, dark-haired woman who was bending over a boy of about Gemma's age. The boy was lying motionless on a thin straw mattress. The woman straightened up with a weary sigh. Then she threaded her way through the crowded hold to where Gemma, Staunton and Tate were standing.

"Good day to you, Mistress Tate," said Staunton stiffly.

The woman nodded to Staunton and smiled weakly at Tate. "Have you brought any food, my dear?" she said.

Tate shook his head. "Not today, but we will try again tomorrow. If it be God's will, we will find some. We must trust in his goodness and mercy."

The woman did not reply.

Tate peered around at the prone and groaning figures. "What news, my dear?"

She shook her head. "Young William Rochdale is even weaker. I fear he may not last the night."

"And our own Priscilla?"

Mrs Tate's face looked grey and haggard. She led Tate and the others over to a small mattress where a tiny child lay motionless, staring up at the ceiling.

"No better, my dear," Mrs Tate replied. "The fever is passed, but unless she has nourishment..." She sighed, as if that was a hopeless wish.

Gemma looked down at the tiny figure. The little girl's eyes turned to Gemma. They were wide and blue in her thin face and seemed full of a sadness so deep that it was beyond tears. It's Priscilla Tate! thought Gemma. The baby from the museum: *infant daughter of...*

Gemma felt tears of her own welling up.

Someone cried out from the far side of the deck. Mrs Tate gave a sorrowful sigh. The cry came again, shriller and more despairing. Mrs Tate turned and began to make her way over the bodies in the direction of the cries.

Tate looked down at Gemma. "My wife needs help tending the sick – go and assist her."

As she turned to follow Mrs Tate, Gemma heard Tate whisper: "Be gentle with the lad, Captain Staunton. His wits are muddled from the blow. He must have been living in the woods, or we would have found him sooner. When he is recovered he might be able to tell us more – who knows, he might even be able to lead us to where there is game." He paused. Staunton muttered something that Gemma didn't catch.

"No, Captain," Tate replied. "I believe he will be able to help us – and let us be honest with each other. Do we not need all the help we can get – from wherever that help may come?"

I *can* help you, thought Gemma, as she picked her way over the restless bodies to where Mrs Tate was kneeling beside a young girl. And I *will* help you – all of you!

3. The Ambush

Gemma clambered up the ladder and through the hatch. The sun was rising. She felt absolutely exhausted. Throughout the whole of the long night, she and Mrs Tate had gone from mattress to mattress with a bucket of drinking water and a wooden ladle, trying to ease the parched throats of the groaning fever-sufferers. It was morning at last. Everyone below deck was still alive, but poor little Priscilla Tate looked weaker than ever, and she was deathly pale.

At the far end of the deck from Gemma stood Captain Staunton. He was looking thoughtfully up at the sky, trying to work out what sort of weather they might expect. There was no time to lose; she would have to talk to him before the day's hunting party set out.

Staunton still hadn't noticed her. Gemma took the booklet about the Pioneer Village from her trouser pocket.

She thumbed quickly through it, scanning the pages for one particular passage. At last she found it; it was a passage from Tate's own journal:

...they, digging up, found Indian baskets filled with corn, and some in ears, fair and good, of diverse colours which seemed to them a very goodly sight (having never seen any such before)...

But where had they found the corn? Gemma frantically scanned the next page and the next. It didn't say where! Gemma stuffed the booklet back into her pocket, angry and frustrated. How could she convince the captain if she didn't know where they should look? But she had to try – for the sake of little Priscilla and all of the others, she had to try. She took a deep breath.

"Captain Staunton!" she called out.

Staunton turned around. "Ah, the castaway! It seems to me that blow to your head has robbed you of your manners, boy. If I had the keeping of you, I would see if a few licks of the strap wouldn't bring back your memory of how to behave!"

"I don't understand – " Gemma began.

"That I can see!" snapped back Staunton. "So I will make myself plain enough to be understood even by a halfwit! Do not presume to hail me, boy, or I promise you, I will not spare the rod on you should I ever get the chance!"

The captain turned furiously on his heel and began to walk away.

Gemma was appalled. Just when she needed to win him over, she seemed to have insulted Staunton. And it wasn't an idle threat; she knew that Staunton was perfectly capable of carrying out his threats.

She turned back towards the stern of the ship. She would let him cool off, then try again. As she reached the hatchway, Gemma heard the groans coming up from the hold. She thought again of the weary night helping Mrs Tate tend the sick. She remembered the stick-thin limbs of the half-starved children, and how they wept with hunger.

She turned back. No, she thought, now I have to try again – it's too important. Somehow I've *got* to make him listen. If I don't, little Priscilla Tate and the other Pilgrims are going to die. She knew she had to make the stubborn Staunton listen to what she had to say. Threats or no threats, she would have to risk it!

Gemma turned and hurried after Staunton. "I do apologise most sincerely, Captain Staunton," she said as she caught up with him. "You are quite right, I have behaved rudely. But it's only because I want to help."

"Help? *You?*..." Staunton's voice was full of scorn. "How can a halfwit like you help us, boy?"

"I-I know where you can get food," said Gemma, a little uncertainly.

"Do you mean game?" asked Staunton. "Do you know feeding and watering places – eh, lad?"

"No," replied Gemma. "But I know where you can find corn."

"*Corn?* At *this* time of year?"

Staunton's momentary interest turned to a sneer of contempt at the word corn. "There is no corn. You *have* lost your wits, boy. Be off – "

"Honestly, I *do* know." Gemma was almost pleading. "The Indians bury some of their grain in baskets in the ground. We must take shovels with us and dig."

"Dig?" Staunton couldn't believe what he was hearing. "The ground is like stone, boy. If anything is buried out there, it will have to wait until spring."

"No, please listen to me," said Gemma desperately. "It's buried under loosely-covered mounds. It's easy to dig up. Oh, *please*, let me come with you. I can show you where the stores of grain are."

Staunton looked at her suspiciously. "There's something about you, lad, that is not right – not right at all. I don't believe your story about being shipwrecked, either. Now you say you want to come out with our party and show us these places. How do I know that you're not in league with the savages, and will not lead us into a trap where we may be killed, and all our weapons and clothes taken?"

"No, no, *no!*" Gemma shook her head forcefully. "I'm not going to cause you any harm. I just want to help you, and the Tates, and their poor baby."

Staunton didn't say anything for a long while. He stood and stared at Gemma with narrowed eyes, as if trying to read her thoughts.

After what seemed an eternity, he grunted curtly. "You may come," he said. "But only because we need every able-bodied man and youth we can get. However, I am not going to burden the men with shovels and such like, when for all I know this talk of buried grain is just a wild fancy of yours."

Turning his back on Gemma, he stomped to the side of the ship.

"Lower the boats!" he ordered the three sailors who were standing at the side, looking towards the shore.

With an apathy that stopped just short of rudeness, the sailors untied the long boat, which had been lashed upside down by the side of the ship, and let it down. With the help of another two men, they lowered the second boat over the side and into the water.

"Going off a-soldiering are you, Sergeant?" asked one of the sailors.

The others sniggered.

"*Captain*!" snarled Staunton. His face had turned almost as red as his hair and beard. "My rank is *captain*, and we're going in search of food – which no doubt you will be more than grateful for."

"What we need is to be away and back to England while we're still able," murmured one of the sailors rapidly, almost under his breath. The words were clearly audible, but it was impossible to tell who had spoken. Staunton decided to ignore the insult, and turned his back on the sailors. But Gemma could see that his face was scarlet with rage.

One by one, the shore party clambered over the side and settled themselves in the two boats that bobbed beside *The Antelope*, like ducklings beside a huge mother duck. The sailors swarmed down after the Pilgrims, then they cast off and rowed briskly for the shore.

When they reached the beach, they waded through the shallows and hauled the boats up above the tideline.

Captain Staunton turned to the sailors who were standing in a surly group behind the Pilgrims. "You will stand guard over the boats until we return," he snapped. "The rest of us will go north into the forest in search of game – " he stared at Gemma, "and other food."

He paused, and nodded to Nathan Tate. "Master Tate will take the lead, and I shall protect our rear."

Tate looked at Gemma and smiled. It was very tempting to go with kindly Nathan Tate, who would be leading the foraging party, but it was Captain Staunton who was really in command. It was Captain Staunton she had to convince. Reluctantly, Gemma took her place in the line just in front of Staunton.

They marched in silent single file over the sand dunes, through the sharp-bladed tufts of frosty grass and into the trees that fringed the beach.

The wood was dense and dark. Above
them stretched the tightly-packed trunks of
pines and larches. Following Tate's lead,
they blundered their way through a tangled

mass of dead branches. This wasn't the well-kept woodland of the Pioneer Village; this was a tangled, impenetrable mass. And in the woods, as Gemma knew, there were wolves. She remembered the howls she'd heard the previous day. She knew that wolves wouldn't normally attack people, but if there was no food for the pioneers, there would be nothing for the wolves either. The wolves would be starving and desperate – desperate enough to attack a small group of weary and exhausted Pilgrims. They were pushing their way into deadly danger!

A little way into the wood there was a shout from up ahead: "A path!"

A moment or two later, Gemma found her feet on a firm, well-trodden earth track that snaked its way through the trees. She was just beginning to relax a little when she saw a mound, just a few metres to the right of the path.

"Stop! Stop!" she shouted excitedly. "There! Look! Buried Indian corn!"

The men up ahead stopped. Nathan Tate came hurrying back.

"What is it, lad? What corn?"

"There – " said Gemma, pointing to the mound. "That's where you'll find corn, buried in that mound. I told Captain Staunton – and there it is!"

Tate looked past Gemma to Staunton, who merely shook his head and scowled. "It's all nonsense, Master Tate – one of these tales that travellers tell to amaze simpletons and children. There's nothing in that mound."

"Perhaps we should see, Captain," said Tate gently but firmly. "Master Taylor, Master Lacey – be so good as to dig into that mound that the lad has pointed out to us, and bring me whatever you find."

Two men left the party and began digging with their bare hands. Gemma, Tate and Staunton stood and watched as the men scraped away at the mound. Gradually, they scratched their way down. As the ground got firmer, they took out their knives and used them to dig away at the earth.

After a minute or two, Captain Staunton called across to the men. "Any sign of anything – Corn? Bread? Roast beef?..."

"Nothing, Captain," replied one of the men.

Staunton gave a dismissive snort. "'Tis all nonsense and foolishness, Master Tate! All nonsense and foolishness!"

Tate looked down at Gemma; he shook his head and turned away. Gemma felt her throat tighten as if she was about to cry. Tate's disappointment was much more upsetting to her than Staunton's bad-tempered sneering.

"You may stop digging," he said, walking back towards the path. "There's nothing there."

Suddenly, one of the men gave a shout. "Wait! Master Tate!" he called. "There is something here. Come and look – "

Tate turned around and ran over to where the two men were crouching. He waved in the direction of Gemma and Staunton; they both hurried over.

Sticking out of the sandy soil was what looked like a handle. Kneeling down, they all began to scrabble at the earth. Soon they'd uncovered a large basket, sturdily

51

woven, with a handle on both sides.

They opened the basket which had been fastened at the top. Inside were dried cobs of corn – several kilos of it! It took the combined strength of both Taylor and Lacey – pulling on the handles with all their might – to drag the basket out.

"The answer to our prayers!" Captain Staunton's eyes grew wide.

"Not so quickly, Captain Staunton," objected Tate. "Do not forget, we are Christian men and women – not pirates or savages. We do not steal from other men – no matter who they are. We must obey the Commandments." He turned to face the other members of the foraging party. "We must decide – all of us – what we should do with these things."

To Captain Staunton's obvious disgust, the other Pilgrims began to discuss whether it would be stealing to take the corn. Gemma was amazed that men who were so close to starving could hesitate for even an instant.

Thwock!

Gemma spun around. Sticking out from

a tree trunk just behind her was an arrow.

Thwock!

She and Staunton flung themselves to the ground. There was a cry from up ahead. Gemma lifted her face out of the dirt and saw a man toppling to the ground. He hadn't been as quick as the others; an arrow was sticking out of his right thigh.

Staunton pulled out his musket and fired a shot into the trees. There was a great fluttering and screeching of birds.

Gemma looked up. She could see dark shapes moving swiftly between the densely-packed tree trunks.

Thwock! Thwock!

Two arrows thudded into a tree to Gemma's left; something moved to her right.

Thud!

An arrow embedded itself in the dry leaves a few metres from Gemma's face. She let out a high-pitched shriek of fear.

"Shut up, boy!" snapped Staunton. "This is no time to panic."

But Gemma could hear the fear in his voice, too.

She glanced up to see ghostly grey shapes moving silently through the woods, but this time to the left.

Whooosh – thwock!

Whooosh – thwock!

The Indians were circling the small group of Pilgrims and firing at will.

"This way!" bellowed Staunton. "Quickly!"

He squirmed deeper into the undergrowth, and Gemma crawled frantically after him. He crouched by a tree trunk, reloaded and repacked his musket, and fired a second shot – this time into the clump of trees where the last arrows had come from. Once again, there was a great commotion of birds in the trees, but no sounds of running feet.

Staunton reloaded.

"How many of them are there?" Gemma gasped.

Before Staunton could answer, she saw a shadow flicker amongst the undergrowth far over to their right.

"They're over there!" she yelled, pointing wildly.

Bang!
Thud! Thud!
Two arrows flew from behind them and landed in the tiny gap that lay between Staunton and Gemma.

They both squirmed in the dirt. Arrows were flying at them from every side.

"Quick, boy!" Staunton grabbed the collar of Gemma's jacket and dragged her round to the far side of the tree.

"Shout, boy! Come on – *shout!*" bellowed Staunton.

"Why?"

"Just do as I say! Make it sound like a war-cry. We might scare them off, or they might think we are more than we are. Go on, lad – *shout!*"

Gemma and Staunton yelled at the tops of their voices. Staunton reloaded his gun and fired it into the air. Their yells were joined by shouts from the others. Soon the woods rang with the wild whooping of the Pilgrims, the calls of terrified birds and the crash of Staunton's musket as he frantically loaded and reloaded as fast as he could.

Gemma looked around, keeping her head as low as possible. She peered into the dense, dark forest, looking for any hint of movement in the shadows that surrounded them. They shouted for several more minutes, but the arrows had stopped.

"Have they gone?" panted Gemma, exhausted.

"Maybe," replied Staunton warily. "Or they might have gone back to their village to get others. That could have been just the beginning. Either way, we can't wait here for them to catch us." He cupped his hands around his mouth. "Back to the boats!" he yelled. "Back to the boats!"

Gemma and Staunton watched and waited as the rest of the group crawled through the undergrowth towards them. Two of the men half-carried and half-dragged the wounded Pilgrim. His face was now a ghastly, pale grey colour, from shock.

The air around them was heavy with fear as they crept back along the track towards the beach. Every few metres Staunton held up his hand, and everyone froze, listening for the sounds of movement in the dark woods. Eventually, they reached the sparser trees which fringed the beach. Still under cover of the woods, they stopped to catch their breath while Staunton scouted a little way ahead.

"The boats are untouched," he reported, after crawling back. "I could see the sailors lounging on the beach as if they hadn't a care in the world. Follow me, but keep your heads down. We aren't out of danger yet!"

Gemma suddenly remembered the purpose of the expedition, the whole reason for all the danger.

"What about the food?" she asked. "The corn – ?"

They had dropped the basket when they had been attacked.

Staunton exploded with anger. "Damn your corn, you halfwit!" he bawled. "Let's be out of here before those savages kill us all!"

4. Caught in a Trap

Later that day, William Penney, one of Nathan Tate's servants, died. With the help of the sailors, they sewed a length of canvas around his body. In the grey light, all those who were fit enough gathered on deck. Nathan Tate said a few simple prayers over the body, then they slid the weighted canvas bundle over the side and into the dark waters.

As dusk approached, the foraging party gathered on deck. Thick grey cloud sat low over both land and sea. The Pilgrims were silent as they took their places in the boats. They all knew the dangers they faced, but they had no choice. They could either search for food and risk another Indian attack, or they could stay on board ship and starve.

Once again, Gemma sat in the prow of the leading boat. Captain Staunton no longer watched her every move, nor did he keep a loaded musket in his hand. But his face was tense and unsmiling, and he stared at the shoreline as if he were expecting to see hostile Indians waiting for them.

Nathan Tate steered them to the northern end of the bay, to a small, sheltered cove with a gently-sloping sandy beach. He was avoiding the broad, open beach where they had landed that morning. Gemma could see why; the small cove would be much easier to defend if they had to make another run for it.

Mrs Tate had given Gemma some old clothes, which she was wearing over her own to keep out the biting cold. Gemma suspected that they had belonged to Will Penney, but didn't want to ask. She sat in the bottom of the boat and pulled the borrowed leather jerkin tightly around her. The wind felt even colder than before, and she was exhausted. She had tried to sleep on the boat, but had been kept awake by the feeble crying of little Priscilla Tate. The child was obviously getting weaker and weaker. If she didn't get proper food soon...

"Prepare to land!" barked Captain Staunton.

There was a grating sound and then a sharp jolt. The boat had run aground in the sandy shallows of the cove. The rowers leaped out and hauled the boat up the beach. Sentries were picked, and once again Tate led the party into the wood. After the earlier ambush, all but two of the men carried muskets.

This was a good opportunity to take another look at the little Pioneer Village booklet. Gemma groped beneath the borrowed breeches and pulled it out of her jeans pocket. She squinted at it in the twilight.

But for meeting the friendly Indian Squanto, the settlers would not have survived that first winter. Despite attacks by hostile Indians, they came to trust Squanto and his tribe, and rely on their advice on planting and harvesting crops like Indian corn.

Squanto had been a servant in London, before returning to Massachusetts, and could speak perfect English.

"Don't daydream, lad!" she heard a rough voice growl behind her. Gemma hurriedly pushed the crumpled booklet into the waistband of her breeches. "Keep your eyes peeled for danger. You never know when the savages might attack!"

Gemma turned around and saw Staunton behind her.

Somehow the settlers had to be persuaded to seek help from the Indians – before it was too late for little Priscilla Tate. That meant in the next day or two, Gemma knew. She took a deep breath; this was her opportunity to convince Staunton.

"But surely not all Indians are savages, Captain Staunton – are they? I mean, you could learn things from them…"

"Learn things? What do you mean, boy?"

"Well, you could learn how to plant corn and – and – " Gemma faltered under Staunton's glare.

"And what do you know about it?" Staunton demanded.

"But it's true, isn't it?" persisted Gemma.

"If you could meet some friendly Indians – say, some that could speak English...?"

"*Friendly* Indians?" Staunton was astonished. "What friendly Indians? There are no friendly Indians, boy. Look how they ambushed us earlier! You go and tell Master Thwaite – he that was shot by those murderous savages – you go tell him about your friendly Indians!"

He paused, struggling to control his temper. "If I see any Indians," his eyes narrowed with hatred, "this is what they'll get!" He brandished his musket in the air, then stomped off, leaving Gemma alone at the back of the line.

Gemma could feel tears of frustration prick at her eyes. It wasn't fair! She was trying to save them from starvation and disease, and Staunton wouldn't listen to her.

Gemma turned her head away and pressed her clenched fists into her eyes, trying to force back the tears. She turned her back on the line of marching Pilgrims. No one will ever take me seriously if they see me crying, she thought. She waited for a minute or two. Then she took a couple of deep breaths and looked up again.

All she could see were trees. She felt a sudden panic: there was no sign of anyone else! The others had marched off and left her, and now she was all alone in the forest!

Gemma tried to control her fear. They can't have gone far, she thought. She tried to remember which way they were going, but the forest looked dark and featureless, and there was no sign of a path.

Suddenly there was a rustle to her right. Gemma spun around. She couldn't see anything, but she knew someone was there – or could it be a some*thing*? With a sinking dread she remembered the wolves she had heard. There was a noise behind her; a twig snapped. She turned around. Then came another noise, like a footfall, to her left. She was surrounded! She knew what was happening; something was circling around her, closing in on her, getting ready to attack!

With a shriek, Gemma ran blindly away from the last sound and into the woods. Twigs scratched at her face and caught in her hair, but she tore herself free and rushed on. She hurtled across a small clearing and plunged between two trees which seemed to mark the beginning of a path. As she darted between them, she noticed that there was something odd about one of them; it was strangely bent, but...

Crash!

The bent tree flew upwards, and suddenly Gemma was jerked off her feet. It was a trap! Her foot had caught in a noose and freed the tree, which had sprung back up, catapulting her into the air.

Gemma hung upside down in the air, careering into the thin trunk of the tree. The blow knocked all the air out of her lungs, so that instead of shouting for help, all she could do was fight to draw her breath.

5. Squanto to the Rescue

As Gemma's breath came back in painful sobs, she opened her eyes. The world was upside down. Her right leg was held tightly in a noose that was lashed to the very top of the sapling.

"Hel-!"

Her cry was cut short by a large, muscular hand covering her mouth. She gazed terrified into the face of an Indian. It was painted with broad orange-red streaks down both cheeks. Grinning broadly, the Indian drew a flint knife out of his belt and waved it in Gemma's face. She tried in vain to yell for help as the knife cut through the leather thong that kept her dangling in midair, and she tumbled to the ground.

The Indian dragged Gemma to her feet, but kept his hand firmly clamped over her mouth. She gazed up into his face. His black hair was shaved above his ears and cropped short on top of his head, so that it looked like a thick pelt. He looked like a kind of wild creature – some sort of red badger? No, thought Gemma, something much more fierce: a wolverine!

This wasn't one of the friendly Indians she had been trying to persuade Staunton to look for; this was Staunton's idea of what an Indian was. This was a fighter, a warrior, and the paint on his face was intended to terrify his enemies.

Keeping his hand over Gemma's mouth, the warrior pulled her backwards through a thicket of dense undergrowth and into a clearing to one side of the track. Two others were waiting in the clearing. Both wore the same face paint as Gemma's captor, and both were carrying bows.

They stared at Gemma. Then one of them pointed to her neck. He stepped forward and grasped her bead necklace. His eyes blazed with anger. My necklace! thought Gemma. Why is that making them so angry?

Without warning, there was a gentle *whoosh*, and the Indian to Gemma's right let out a cry. An arrow was jutting out of the thick muscle at the top of his right arm. *Whoosh!* Another arrow skimmed over his head and vanished into the trees.

Whooosh! And another!

Gemma was flung to the ground.

Whooosh!

She heard the sounds of rushing feet crashing through the undergrowth. She flattened herself against the dirt. The rushing and crashing stopped and Gemma heard feet approaching her. She kept as still as she could. She sensed that there were three, maybe four people standing over her.

"Do not fear, young sir," she heard a voice say in strangely-accented English. "You are safe now."

Very slowly, Gemma raised her head, pushed herself up, and looked around. She was indeed surrounded by Indians, but these Indians looked different. Their hair was tied back tightly but not shaved, and their faces were unpainted. A tall man stepped forward.

"Do not fear," he repeated. To her amazement, he held out a hand to help

Gemma to her feet. "I wish to be your friend!"

At the word friend, Gemma felt all the terror that had been building up inside her, burst out like a rush of flood water. Without being able to stop herself, she fell to her knees, clinging to the Indian's arm and sobbing uncontrollably.

Gently, the Indian helped Gemma to her feet. Her sobbing subsided into hiccupy coughs and she wiped her nose on her sleeve.

"Come," he said, in a calm voice. "We must not stay here too long, it is not safe. The others may return soon."

He began to lead her along a track through the woods. The other Indians fell into a silent line behind them.

"So it is a milady, not a milord?" said the English-speaking Indian. He smiled down at Gemma.

"Sorry?" said Gemma.

"You are a girl, not a boy," said the Indian.

"How do you know?" asked Gemma, suprised. She had got so used to her disguise by now, it was a shock to discover that her real identity was so obvious to a complete stranger.

"English boys do not cry like that – easily and openly – even when they are hurt or frightened. They have to play the brave soldier with the stiff upper lip – so!" The Indian pulled a peculiar, stiff face. They both laughed. "This I know," he continued. "I lived among the English for two years. I got to know their customs. But they seem still a very strange people to me."

Gemma gazed up at him. It seemed too much of a coincidence...but it could only be *him*! Living with the English; speaking her language.

"What is the matter?" asked the Indian. "Why do you stare at me like that?"

"It's – it's *you*," said Gemma.

The Indian stopped and looked at her with a puzzled frown.

"Is – is your name Squanto?"

The Indian stared down at her in astonishment.

"How did you know that?" he asked.

Gemma fumbled in the waistband of her breeches and pulled out the creased booklet.

"Your story has been written, and you are famous as a friend of the English," she said.

Squanto started walking again and Gemma followed; together they moved on in silence. The other Indians followed at a slight distance. They seemed afraid of Gemma, and confused by the strange language that she and the tall brave were speaking. It made Gemma feel uncomfortable. Whenever she glanced around, they turned their faces away; they seemed not to want to look at her.

"Tell me," said Squanto slowly, after they had been walking for several minutes. "Why did you pretend to be a boy?"

"Because if they'd known I was a girl, I would not have been allowed out of the ship, and I wouldn't have been able to find you," said Gemma.

"Me?" asked Squanto. "You were looking for *me*?"

Gemma nodded. "Only *you* can save the others, and show them how to farm the land here. The future of this country depends on you!"

Squanto was silent for a minute. "How do you know this?" he asked her slowly.

Gemma held out the booklet again. "It's all written here," she said.

They walked on in silence for another minute or two.

"Thank you for saving me," said Gemma quietly.

Squanto smiled. "It was good luck," he said. "Those men who captured you are from a tribe we have many quarrels with. They attack our villages and steal food from our traps. It was one of our traps you got caught in. We were watching when they came and took you."

"So was it them who attacked us this morning?" asked Gemma.

"It must have been," replied Squanto. "We wish to be friends with the English, so that we can trade with them. But the men who captured you are not as we are – they will kill all strangers, especially those wearing the signs of my tribe." He pointed to Gemma's necklace.

"Your tribe?"

"Yes," said Squanto. "Did you not know?"

Gemma shook her head.

"It is a necklace of my people," replied Squanto. "It is a special necklace. Do you see the pattern of the beads?" Squanto pointed.

Gemma looked down.

"It is a sign that whoever wears this necklace is a – how do the English say? – a magic man. In our tribe, we say that person is a seer." He glanced around. "Do you not see how the others will not walk with us, but stay back? That is out of respect and fear for the wearer of the necklace."

"They think I am a seer?" asked Gemma.

Squanto nodded. "One who can see over the tallest mountains and across the greatest seas – the seas of water, and also the seas of air and fire." He looked at Gemma carefully.

"I – I just found it," said Gemma hesitantly. "In an old box, by the sea. I didn't know it was special in *that* way."

"Such findings are fate," said Squanto. "Your powers must be a great secret in your own country."

Gemma shook her head. "I don't have any special powers, I'm just an ordinary girl. It's – it's the necklace that has the power. I'm not a seer; I'm just a visitor – a traveller."

Squanto nodded. "That is what my

grandfather used to say," he said slowly. "He was a seer. He used to say that it was like a journey – sometimes into the past, sometimes into the future, and sometimes into the Dreamworld. To be given this power is a great gift. My grandfather knew this well. Others used this gift to make themselves more powerful. But my grandfather used to say that such gifts are only to be used for the good of others, never for your own gain or to harm another. I believe you know this, and will use your gifts wisely. Ah – here we are: my village!"

They were standing in a large, open space in the woodland. Clustered together in the middle of the clearing were a number of round huts with curved roofs. The walls and roofs were made from woven mats. The smell of cooking wafting Gemma's way suddenly made her feel dizzy with hunger.

"Come with me," said Squanto. "You must eat."

He led the way to one of the huts, and lifted up a mat which covered a doorway about a metre high. Stooping carefully, Gemma followed Squanto into the hut. A fire was burning in a small pit in the centre, and the smoke was escaping through a large gap in the roof. Instead of rugs or carpets, there were more woven mats laid on the floor. As Gemma's eyes grew accustomed to the darkness, she could see wooden bowls, dishes and plain earthenware pots neatly stacked at the sides of the hut. There were baskets, too, decorated with black and white interwoven threads. A smiling woman, who had been tending a pot that was hanging over the fire, came to greet them.

Squanto murmured something to her that Gemma didn't hear. The woman smiled again and walked back to the pot over the fire. She reached in and ladled something out on to a flat wooden platter, which she handed to Gemma. On the platter were two pieces of casseroled meat which tasted wonderful – sweet and succulent. Gemma ate so quickly that she made herself breathless.

"Good?" asked Squanto, when she had

finished.

"Yes!" replied Gemma. "Thank you!"

"Now, if you are to meet your friends again, we must make haste," continued Squanto. "The sky is nearly dark, and they will be leaving for their ship."

6. Surrendering the White Flag

Squanto led Gemma out of the hut. Six other Indians were waiting for them outside. Three of them were carrying large, covered baskets woven from dried grasses. Squanto hastily said a few words to the men, and led the way back to the woodland track. Despite the growing gloom, they sped along the forest paths until they reached the shore.

The settlers were already pushing the boat down to the sea.

"Wait!" shouted Gemma, waving frantically. "Wait! Look! I've brought help!" She pointed to the small group of Indians that surrounded her.

Staunton looked around. Seeing the Indians, he immediately dropped to one knee and brought his musket up to his shoulder. "Indians!" he yelled. "Ambush!"

He aimed his musket. A shot rang out. The musket ball whistled over Gemma's head and embedded itself in the trunk of a birch tree just behind her.

"No!" screamed Gemma. "We – !" But whatever she was about to say was silenced by Squanto pushing her to the ground and pressing her face down into the sand.

Staunton dodged behind the shelter of the boat to reload. "Load your muskets, men," he shouted to the others, as they struggled with powder, balls and ramrods. "Fire at will!"

A ragged outburst of shots crashed harmlessly through the branches behind Gemma and the Indians.

"Back to the woods!" shouted Squanto, squirming backwards towards the shelter of the trees, pulling Gemma with him.

"No!" screamed Gemma through a

mouthful of sand. "This isn't what should happen!"

Another volley crashed into the branches just above their heads. She and Squanto ducked. The Pilgrims' aim was getting better.

"Mr Tate!" she shouted. "Please listen to me! I've brought help! Please stop shooting and let me explain – "

"Ready... *Fire!*" came the reply from Staunton.

"Captain Staunton, please listen! It *isn't* an ambush!" pleaded Gemma in the silence after the next volley. "I've brought an Indian who is a friend of Englishmen. He speaks English! He's lived in England."

"Don't you think – ?" she heard Nathan Tate begin.

"It's a trap!" she heard Staunton shout. "There's no such thing as an English-speaking Indian. The lad has betrayed us to the savages! Ready, aim, *fire!*"

More shots crashed into the foliage behind Gemma and Squanto.

"Let us go back," said Squanto. "This is hopeless, they will never listen. Why should we risk ourselves to help people who do not want our help? Maybe they deserve to die."

"No!" Gemma was horrified. "It's not just Captain Staunton and the men who need help – think about the women and the children. They don't deserve to die just because one man is too stubborn to listen – do they?"

Squanto looked across at Gemma and shrugged. "Maybe not, but if we cannot even make ourselves heard, there is nothing we can do to help them."

There was another crash of musket fire. The pair ducked down again.

Gemma was almost beside herself with frustration. She was bringing the Pilgrims help, for themselves and for their loved ones, and this was how they responded – with musket balls! If only she could explain, but it was impossible to be heard over the crash of musket fire – and in any case, she thought, how can you have a reasoned conversation with someone whose only wish is to shoot you down! If only there was something she could say or do to make them stop – just long enough to be able to explain.

Another volley of musket fire crashed into the trees behind Gemma and Squanto.

"They don't seem to have noticed that no one's firing back," said Squanto bitterly.

"Sorry?" said Gemma. Something in Squanto's words gave Gemma the glimmerings of an idea. "Could you say that again?"

"I said: they don't seem to have noticed that no one's firing back," said Squanto. "They don't seem to have realised that no one has attacked them at all. *They* are the ones who are shooting at unarmed men."

It was true! thought Gemma. In their hurry to defend themselves against another attack, the Pilgrims hadn't noticed that it was *they* who were the aggressors. But Gemma knew that the Pilgrims *weren't* aggressive people. Even if Captain Staunton was quite willing to shoot first and ask questions later, the other Pilgrims were men of peace; men who believed in the Ten Commandments. She remembered how they'd worried about whether taking the Indians' corn might be theft. They wouldn't shoot people, even Indians, in cold blood – would they?

There was a lull in the firing, as the ragged musketeers struggled to reload their cumbersome weapons.

"No one is attacking you!" Gemma shrieked at the top of her voice. "Can't you see? *No one is attacking you*! You are shooting at unarmed men! If you kill one of us it will be *murder*!"

She paused, struggling to remember the test that they'd had on the Ten Commandments in an RE lesson months ago. She mentally went through the list until she came to the right one. If anything might convince the Pilgrims to listen to her, this would.

"Don't you remember the sixth Commandment?" she shouted. "*Thou Shalt Not Kill*!"

There was a long silence.

Gemma held her breath, waiting.

Then a voice from the Pilgrims' line shouted: "Hold your fire!"

It wasn't Staunton who had yelled the order, but Nathan Tate.

There was silence. "Is that you, lad?" she heard Tate call.

"Yes," shouted Gemma.

"And you have Indians with you?"

"Yes," Gemma called back. "But it's not what Captain Staunton thinks. Nobody wants to harm you – honestly! All they want to do is help you – all of you. They can give you food and show you where to hunt and where to find berries to eat."

She waited for a reply. She could hear the low murmur of voices drifting across the sand; there was obviously a hasty conference going on between Tate and Staunton.

"How can we be sure?" shouted Tate. "How can we trust you?"

"You have been shooting at us, but no one has shot at *you* – isn't that proof enough?" Gemma shouted back. "These are not the Indians who ambushed us before. If they were – well, I wouldn't be here, would I?"

She paused. "They saved my life, and

they can save your lives – and the lives of your wives and children. Please listen to me – *please trust me!*" she begged.

She forced a hand under the waistband of the borrowed breeches and into a pocket of her jeans underneath. After a struggle, she managed to pull out a large, white handkerchief. Picking up a twig from nearby, Gemma tied the handkerchief to it.

"We'll meet under a flag of truce!" she shouted. She waved the flag above her, so that the Pilgrims could clearly see it.

"Be careful," whispered Squanto, as Gemma got to her knees. "I do not trust them!"

"Think of your families, your wives and your children!" she repeated. "Mr Tate! *Think of Priscilla!*"

Gemma clambered unsteadily to her feet. In the distant gloom, she could make out Nathan Tate standing behind the rowing boat, with Captain Staunton to his right.

She took a tentative step forward. This was a moment of real history, and she was helping to make it! She waved her home-made flag and began to walk slowly forward. Staunton and the others kept their muskets pointed at Gemma as she walked towards them. She swallowed hard. She knew that Staunton was skilled with weapons, but the others were clearly nervous and very fearful. She hoped against hope that they kept their heads.

Gemma looked towards the armed Pilgrims who were lined up like a firing squad less than fifty metres in front of her. As she got closer, she saw a man to the right tense up; his finger was ready on the trigger.

"Please," she whispered under her breath, "don't panic."

She paused, and looked around. Squanto was standing to her right, a pace or two behind. He was holding his arms out to his sides, with his hands palm upwards to show that he was unarmed. He took a few paces forward until he was standing in front of her.

"I come without weapons – I come in peace," he said slowly.

Gemma could see amazement on the faces of the Pilgrims.

"I have lived among the English," continued Squanto, "and I am their friend. I bring you greetings from my tribe – and gifts!"

He turned his head back to the waiting Indians.

One of them took two paces forward, then stopped. Like Squanto, he held his arms out to his sides, but from each hand dangled the carcass of a plump rabbit. There was a sharp intake of breath from the ragged line of Pilgrims.

Slowly, Squanto stepped forward. As he did so, Captain Staunton took a step too, musket at the ready. But Nathan Tate put a restraining hand on Staunton's shoulder; he shook his head. Staunton grimaced, but gave way and stepped back.

Tate turned to face Squanto and took two paces towards him. He also had his arms wide and his palms open.

Cautiously, the two men approached each other, a step at a time. They stopped, two paces apart. Squanto looked Tate straight in the eye, then lifted one hand in salute. "God Save The King!" he cried.

7. The Letter

Squanto stood at the side of the ship in the darkness. As Gemma climbed up from below deck, she saw him gazing back towards the shore. Was he considering the future of his land and people, she wondered, or remembering the time he had already spent in the company of Englishmen?

The Pilgrims had fed well on the fresh fish and game which Squanto and the others had brought as gifts. The rabbits were plump and delicious; even the dried cod had tasted good!

Gemma had helped Mrs Tate feed Priscilla a few spoonfuls of broth from the cooked rabbits, mixed with a little corn meal that the Indians had also brought with them. Priscilla had been almost too weak to suck the food off the spoon, but she had managed a little and was now fast asleep. Gemma had done her best; all that she could do now was hope that Priscilla got better.

In return for the food, the Pilgrims had given the Indians a pair of bone-handled knives and a looking glass. The Indians had seemed delighted after their first trade with the Pilgrims, but only Squanto had agreed to come on board the ship to share the meal. Now that it was over, he seemed anxious to return to his people.

Gemma approached him. Squanto turned and tensed, then relaxed again when he saw that it was Gemma.

"Are you nervous, being on the ship?" she asked.

Squanto shrugged. "A little," he said quietly. "The last time I boarded a ship in this bay, I was carried off to England. I didn't see my home or my family for two years." He paused, then added quickly, "Though I do not think your friends will carry me off to England!" He sighed. "And now the English have come back – but not to trade, to settle."

Gemma stood silently by his side, looking up into his dark eyes. She had taken off her leather breeches and jerkin, and wearing just her normal clothes shivered now in the icy wind that buffeted across the deck.

"These are good men – men who can be trusted," continued Squanto. "Even Captain Staunton – he is a fierce warrior, but he is also a man of honour; when he gives his word it is so. But soon others will come who are not men of honour, men who wish to steal from us and cheat us..." The dismal thought ended in a heavy sigh. "You wear the sign of the seer," he said to Gemma, pointing at her necklace. "Is this not true?"

Gemma shuddered. She knew from her history lessons what would happen. As soon as the settlers no longer needed the Indians to show them how to survive in the new land, they would steal the good land and force the Indians to live on barren reservations. Then the settlers would tell themselves that it was the white man's right to take whatever he wanted. Her hand went up to her throat and touched the tiny beads that made up her necklace.

"I shouldn't have this," she said. "It doesn't belong to me, or to my people.

I've got to go back to my own place. I've done what I came to do. This should be yours...here – " She took the necklace from around her neck and pressed it into Squanto's open hand.

The whole world seemed to spin around, faster and faster, and Gemma felt as if she was falling. When the dizziness stopped, she was staring down, not at the wooden deck of *The Antelope*, but at the sunlit, wooden floor at the entrance to the Peacehaven Pioneer museum.

She sat motionless for several minutes, still hearing Squanto's voice:

...others will come who are not men of honour, men who wish to steal from us and cheat us...

What had she done? Had she simply made everything worse?

She stood up and walked slowly back into the large gallery again. The cradle was still in the middle of the floor, as it had been before Gemma had gone on her journey; but something in the glass cabinet caught her eye. She went over and stared in again. Next to the journal and the letters was something that Gemma was sure hadn't been there before: a bead necklace – a very familiar bead necklace.

Then Gemma looked for the first time at the yellowing letters beside the journal. One was dated March 1643 and was in Nathan Tate's handwriting. It was to Mrs Priscilla Proctor. It was full of advice on when to plant certain crops and when to harvest them. Gemma skipped to the end of the letter; it was signed: *Your loving father, Nathan Tate.*

Mrs *Priscilla* Proctor! Priscilla Proctor and Priscilla Tate were the same person! Priscilla had lived and had gone on to marry!

Maybe, thought Gemma, maybe I *did* do some good after all.

"*That's* where you are!" Her father was standing in the doorway. "We were wondering where you'd got to. Come and have a look in here – " he pointed towards the next room. "They've got a display of arms and armour that belonged to the original settlers. They've got Captain Staunton's musket and helmet – all sorts!"

Gemma shook her head. "No, thanks," she said. "I don't think I want to look at guns and things. I think I might just go outside in the sunshine."

"All right," said Dad, "but don't wander off and get into mischief."

"Oh no," said Gemma. "I wouldn't do anything like that!"